WE?

A TALE OF LOVE AND DESTINY

ROHAN SAHA

Made with ♥ on the Notion Press Platform
www.notionpress.com

Dedicated to my loved ones

Contents

We?

"We?" is a beautiful love story that showcases the journey of two individuals, Emma and Drake, as they fall in love and learn to navigate through various challenges. The story begins with their first encounter, where they both feel an instant connection but are hesitant to take it further. However, as fate would have it, they bump into each other again and decide to go on their first date.

As they go on their first few dates, they begin to develop feelings for each other, but doubts start to creep in. Emma begins to wonder if Drake is really the one for her, while Drake starts to worry about their communication and distance issues. Despite these doubts, they both realize that they want to make it work and decide to give their relationship a chance.

However, as they navigate through their relationship, they face various obstacles like distance, communication, and personal differences. Despite these obstacles, they continue to grow together and face unexpected twists. They take their relationship to the next level and pass the big test, which brings them even closer together.

The story ends with them happily ever after, getting married, going on their honeymoon, and planning their future together. The proposal is a beautiful moment where Drake surprises Emma with a ring, and they plan their wedding together. They both have bachelor/bachelorette parties with their friends and family, and finally, they have a beautiful wedding day where they exchange vows and start their life together as a married couple. They then go on their honeymoon, where they have an amazing time together, and start planning their future together.

Overall, "We?" is a heartwarming love story that shows how two people can come together and overcome obstacles to find happiness and love.

Title Significance

The title "We?" can carry a lot of significance, depending on the context of the story. In general, the title implies a question about the relationship between two or more people, and suggests that there may be some uncertainty or doubt about that relationship.

If the story is a love story, for example, the title might suggest that the two characters are questioning whether they are truly compatible, or whether they should be together at all. The question mark in the title adds to this sense of uncertainty, and implies that the characters are struggling to find answers.

Alternatively, the title "We?" could also suggest a story about a group of people who are trying to work together towards a common goal, but are facing obstacles or disagreements. In this case, the title might suggest that the group is questioning whether they can truly come together and achieve their goal, or whether their differences are too great to overcome.

Overall, the title "We?" can carry a lot of weight and significance, and can set the tone for a story that explores themes of relationships, doubt, and uncertainty.

1

First Encounters

Emma had always been a small-town girl. She grew up in a tight-knit community, surrounded by people who knew her by name and where she felt comfortable. But she had always felt that she was meant for something more than just the simple life she had grown up with. That's why when she got a job offer in the city, she jumped at the chance to start a new chapter in her life.

On her first morning in town, Emma decided to treat herself to a cup of coffee at a nearby cafe. She was feeling both excited and nervous about starting a new job and a new life in the big city.

As she waited in line, she noticed a tall, dark-haired man who caught her eye. He was dressed in a sharp suit and had an air of confidence that drew her attention.

When he turned around and caught her gaze, he smiled and said, "Good morning."

Emma felt her heart skip a beat as she smiled back and replied, "Good morning."

They struck up a conversation, and she learned that his name was Drake. He was a lawyer who had lived in the city for several years.

As they chatted, Emma found herself drawn to his easy smile and charming personality. She couldn't help but notice the way his eyes crinkled at the corners when he laughed or the way he held himself with a confident ease. He was everything she wasn't – bold, confident, and unafraid to take risks.

When it was her turn to order, Emma nervously stumbled over her words, which made Drake laugh and put her at ease. She found herself opening up to him, sharing stories about her life back in the small town, and about how she was looking forward to starting fresh in the city.

As they left the cafe, Drake asked for her number, and Emma eagerly gave it to him. She felt a flutter of excitement in her stomach as he walked away, and she knew that there was something special about this chance encounter.

Over the next few days, Emma couldn't get Drake out of her head. She would catch herself daydreaming about him, wondering what it would be like to see him again.

Then, one evening, her phone rang, and it was him. He asked if she wanted to grab a drink after work, and Emma eagerly said yes.

They met at a trendy bar downtown, and the chemistry between them was undeniable. They talked and laughed for hours, and Emma felt like she had known Drake for years. It was like they were two pieces of a puzzle that fit perfectly together.

As the night wore on, they walked out into the cool night air. Emma shivered, and Drake took off his jacket and draped it over her shoulders. They walked down the empty street, arm in arm, and Emma felt like she was walking on air.

When they got to her apartment, Drake leaned in to kiss her, and Emma's heart raced. The kiss was electric, and it was clear that they both felt a strong connection.

As the days turned into weeks, Emma and Drake went on more dates, exploring the city and getting to know each other better. They learned that they had a lot in common, from their love of good food to their shared passion for travel.

But as they grew closer, Emma began to worry that Drake wasn't ready for a serious relationship. He seemed content to keep things casual, and Emma didn't want to get hurt.

She confided in her best friend, who urged her to be honest with Drake about her feelings. "You'll never know what could have been if you don't take a chance," her friend said.

So Emma decided to take a risk and tell Drake how she felt. They sat down over coffee one afternoon, and Emma nervously told him that she wanted more.

2

First Dates

Drake was surprised when Emma expressed her desire for a more serious relationship. He had been enjoying spending time with her, but he wasn't sure if he was ready to commit to anything long-term.

But as he looked into her eyes, he saw the sincerity and vulnerability there, and he knew that he didn't want to let her go.

"I understand your concerns, Emma, and I want you to know that I care about you a lot," Drake said. "Let's take this slow and see where it goes."

Emma felt relieved and happy that Drake was willing to give their relationship a chance. They agreed to continue seeing each other, but to take things one step at a time.

Their first date after this conversation was to a fancy Italian restaurant. Emma had always loved Italian food, and she was excited to try this new place. As they sat across from each other, enjoying their meal, Emma felt grateful to have someone like Drake in her life.

They talked about everything and anything, from their childhoods to their dreams for the future. Emma found herself drawn to Drake's ambition and drive, but also to his ability to make her laugh.

After dinner, they walked along the waterfront, enjoying the cool breeze and the sound of the waves. Drake took her hand, and Emma felt her heart flutter with excitement. They stopped to watch the sunset, and Drake pulled her close, kissing her gently.

As they continued to see each other, Emma and Drake fell deeper in love. They went on more dates, exploring the city and trying new things. They went to museums, concerts, and even took a cooking class together.

Emma loved spending time with Drake, but she couldn't help but feel a little nervous. She knew that she was falling for him quickly, and she didn't want to scare him off.

One day, Drake surprised her with tickets to a weekend getaway to a secluded cabin in the woods. Emma was thrilled at the idea of spending time alone with him, but she was also a little nervous. She had never been on a trip like this with anyone before.

As they drove up to the cabin, Emma couldn't believe how beautiful it was. The cabin was surrounded by trees, and there was a lake nearby. It was the perfect place to relax and unwind.

Over the weekend, Emma and Drake went on hikes, cooked meals together, and cuddled up by the fire. They talked for hours, getting to know each other even better. Emma felt like she was living in a fairy tale, and she didn't want the weekend to end.

As they packed up to leave on Sunday, Drake took Emma by the hand and looked into her eyes. "Emma, I know we haven't been seeing each other for very long, but I feel like we have something really special here," he said.

Emma's heart skipped a beat. She knew what was coming next.

"I want to be with you, Emma. I want to make this official. Will you be my girlfriend?" he asked.

Tears welled up in Emma's eyes as she nodded her head, unable to speak. Drake hugged her tightly, and Emma felt like she was floating on air.

As they drove back to the city, Emma felt like her life had changed forever. She was no longer just a small-town girl trying to make it in the big city. She was part of a team now – "we," as Drake had said – and she knew that together, they could conquer anything.

3

Doubts

As the weeks passed, Emma and Drake continued to be happy together. They went on more dates and spent more time together, but Emma couldn't help but feel a nagging sense of doubt in the back of her mind.

She had been hurt in the past, and she was scared that history would repeat itself. She didn't want to get too attached to Drake, only to have him break her heart.

Emma tried to push these thoughts aside and focus on the present moment, but they kept creeping back into her mind.

One evening, as they were snuggled up on the couch watching a movie, Emma couldn't take it anymore. She turned to Drake and blurted out her fears.

"What if this doesn't work out? What if you leave me like everyone else has?"

Drake looked at her with concern in his eyes. "Emma, I would never hurt you like that. I care about you too much."

"But how can you be so sure? What makes our relationship different from all the others that have failed?" Emma asked.

Drake took a deep breath and looked at her with sincerity. "I can't promise you that nothing will ever go wrong. But what I can promise you is that I will always be here for you. No matter what happens, we'll face it together."

Emma felt a wave of relief wash over her. She knew that she had found someone special in Drake, and she didn't want to let her doubts get in the way of their relationship.

Over the next few weeks, Emma tried her best to push her fears aside and enjoy her time with Drake. They went on more dates, took long walks in the park, and even went on a weekend trip to a nearby town.

But the doubts continued to linger in the back of Emma's mind. She tried to talk herself out of them, but they just wouldn't go away.

One day, as they were sitting in a coffee shop, Emma's phone rang. It was her ex-boyfriend, calling to apologize for the way he had treated her in the past.

Emma felt her heart rate skyrocket. She had spent so long trying to forget about her ex, and now he was back in her life.

Drake noticed the change in her demeanor and asked what was wrong. Emma hesitated, not wanting to ruin their day together, but she knew that she had to be honest with him.

"My ex just called me," she said. "He wants to get back together."

Drake looked at her with concern in his eyes. "What do you want to do?"

"I don't know," Emma said. "Part of me still cares about him, but I don't want to hurt you."

Drake took her hand and looked into her eyes. "Emma, I want you to be happy. If that means going back to your ex, then I'll understand. But if you decide to stay with me, then know that I'll always be here for you."

Emma felt a wave of gratitude wash over her. She knew that Drake was the one she wanted to be with, but she also knew that it wouldn't be easy.

Over the next few days, Emma struggled with her decision. She thought about her ex and the life they used to have together, but she also thought about the future she could have with Drake.

Finally, after much deliberation, Emma made her decision. She called her ex and told him that she had moved on and that she was happy with Drake.

It wasn't an easy decision, but it was the right one. Emma knew that she had found something special with Drake, and she didn't want to let it go. Together, they could conquer anything – even her doubts and fears.

4

Confessions

As Emma and Drake's relationship continued to grow, Emma found herself falling deeper in love with him every day. She felt like she could tell him anything, but there was one thing she had been keeping from him.

Emma had always been hesitant to talk about her past. She had experienced a lot of pain and heartbreak, and it was something she preferred to keep buried deep down inside.

But as her feelings for Drake grew stronger, Emma knew that she couldn't keep her secrets from him any longer. She needed to tell him the truth.

One evening, as they were sitting on the couch, Emma mustered up the courage to speak.

"Drake, there's something I need to tell you," she said.

Drake looked at her with concern. "What is it?"

"I've had a rough past," Emma began. "I've been hurt a lot in the past, and it's made me hesitant to open up to people. But with you, it's different. I feel like I can trust you, and I want you to know everything about me."

Drake listened attentively as Emma recounted her past experiences. She talked about the pain she had endured and the ways in which it had shaped her into the person she was today.

As she spoke, Drake held her hand and looked into her eyes with understanding. He didn't judge her for her past; instead, he offered her his unwavering support and love.

"Emma, I'm so sorry for the pain you've been through," he said. "But I want you to know that I love you for who you are, past and all. And I promise to always be here for you, no matter what."

Emma felt a weight lifted off her shoulders. She knew that she had made the right decision in telling Drake the truth, and she was grateful for his love and support.

Over the next few weeks, Emma felt closer to Drake than ever before. They continued to share their deepest fears and desires with each other, and their relationship grew stronger with each passing day.

Emma knew that she had found something special with Drake, and she was excited to see what the future held for them. Together, they could overcome anything – even the pain of their pasts.

5

Obstacles

Despite the strong bond that Emma and Drake shared, they still faced obstacles in their relationship. Emma's past traumas continued to haunt her, and Drake had his own personal struggles to deal with as well.

One of the biggest obstacles they faced was distance. Drake was a traveling doctor, and his job required him to be away from Emma for long periods of time. It was difficult for both of them to be apart, but they tried to make it work by staying in touch through phone calls and video chats.

Another obstacle they faced was their different personalities. Emma was an introvert who enjoyed spending time alone, while Drake was more outgoing and enjoyed being around people. They struggled to find a balance between their different preferences and often found themselves arguing about how to spend their free time.

Despite these challenges, Emma and Drake were determined to make their relationship work. They knew that they loved each other and were willing to put in the effort to overcome any obstacles that came their way.

One day, Emma received a call from her ex-boyfriend, who had been trying to reach her for weeks. Emma was hesitant to answer the call, but she eventually picked up, hoping to put an end to the persistent calls.

As soon as she heard his voice, Emma felt a wave of panic wash over her. Her ex-boyfriend began to berate her, bringing up painful memories from their past together. Emma felt herself spiraling back into the same old negative thought patterns that had haunted her for years.

Drake could sense that something was wrong and asked Emma what was going on. She hesitated at first, not wanting to burden him with her problems, but eventually, she told him everything.

Drake listened patiently, offering words of encouragement and support. He reminded Emma of how much he loved her and how much he believed in their relationship.

With Drake's support, Emma was able to overcome her doubts and fears. She realized that she didn't need to be defined by her past, and that she had the power to shape her own future.

As Emma and Drake worked through their obstacles together, they grew even closer as a couple. They learned to appreciate each other's differences and to support each other through the ups and downs of life. Together, they were unstoppable, and nothing could stand in the way of their love.

6

Making It Work

Emma and Drake had been dating for a few months now, and while they faced some obstacles, they were determined to make their relationship work. They had learned to appreciate each other's differences, and they supported each other through thick and thin.

However, the long-distance aspect of their relationship was still challenging. Drake's job as a traveling doctor required him to be away from Emma for long periods of time, and it was hard on both of them. They missed each other terribly when they were apart and cherished every moment they had together.

Despite the challenges, Emma and Drake made a conscious effort to stay connected. They made sure to text, call, and video chat regularly. They also planned visits whenever they could, and even took trips together to explore new places.

One of their favorite trips was a weekend getaway to a cabin in the woods. They spent the days hiking, enjoying the scenery, and just being together. At night, they cuddled by the fire, talking about their hopes and dreams for the future.

It was during this trip that Emma and Drake began to talk about the possibility of moving in together. They both knew it was a big step, but they were ready to take it.

After a few more discussions, they decided to take the plunge and find a place to live together. It wasn't easy finding a place that met both of their needs, but eventually, they found a cozy apartment in the city that they both loved.

Moving in together was a big adjustment for both Emma and Drake. They had to learn how to compromise and communicate effectively in order to make their new living situation work. They quickly fell into a routine, sharing household chores and making time for each other despite their busy schedules.

As they settled into their new home together, Emma and Drake's love for each other continued to grow. They were each other's support system, cheering each other on through life's challenges and celebrating each other's accomplishments.

They were happy and content, and it seemed that nothing could break the bond they had formed. They had learned that with love, patience, and hard work, anything was possible.

7

Surprises

Emma and Drake had been living together for a few months now, and while they were happy, they were also looking for ways to keep the spark alive in their relationship. They had fallen into a comfortable routine, and they wanted to surprise each other and keep things exciting.

Drake decided to plan a surprise date night for Emma. He knew that she loved live music, so he bought tickets to a concert of her favorite band. He also made reservations at a fancy restaurant and arranged for a chauffeured car to take them there.

Emma was completely surprised and thrilled by Drake's thoughtfulness. She couldn't believe how much effort he had put into planning the perfect evening for her. They enjoyed a delicious dinner and danced the night away at the concert, feeling like they were falling in love all over again.

Emma also wanted to surprise Drake, so she decided to plan a weekend trip to a place he had always wanted to visit. She secretly booked a cabin in the mountains and packed their bags for a weekend getaway.

When they arrived, Drake was amazed at the beautiful scenery and the cozy cabin. Emma had also planned some fun activities for them, like hiking and horseback riding. They spent the weekend exploring the outdoors and enjoying each other's company, feeling grateful for the surprises that kept their relationship fresh and exciting.

As they continued to surprise each other with thoughtful gestures and romantic gestures, Emma and Drake realized that these surprises were what kept their love strong. They learned that it wasn't just about the big grand gestures, but also the small and thoughtful acts of love that made a difference in their relationship.

They felt lucky to have found each other, and they knew that they would continue to surprise and support each other for years to come. They were each other's greatest surprise, and they wouldn't have it any other way.

8

Growing Together

Emma and Drake had been together for a while now, and their relationship was growing stronger every day. They had been through their fair share of challenges, but they had come out on the other side even more committed to each other.

One of the challenges they faced was dealing with their individual goals and aspirations. Emma was passionate about her career as a graphic designer, while Drake was focused on building his own business. They both supported each other's dreams, but they also had to learn how to balance their individual ambitions with their relationship.

To help them navigate this challenge, they started scheduling weekly "check-ins" where they would talk about their goals and how they could support each other. They also made a point to celebrate each other's successes, no matter how big or small.

As they grew together, Emma and Drake also found themselves learning more about each other's interests and hobbies. Emma had always loved cooking, but she had never really shared that with Drake. So, she decided to surprise him by preparing a gourmet dinner from scratch one night. Drake was blown away by her culinary skills and loved the fact that she was sharing something so personal with him.

In turn, Drake introduced Emma to his love of hiking and the outdoors. He took her on a challenging hike to a stunning lookout point, and Emma was amazed by the beauty of nature. She appreciated how Drake was pushing her out of her comfort zone and showing her new things.

Through these experiences, Emma and Drake learned that growing together meant embracing each other's differences and supporting each other's passions. They also discovered that being open to trying new things together was key to keeping their relationship fresh and exciting.

As they continued to grow together, Emma and Drake felt more connected than ever before. They knew that they were each other's biggest cheerleaders and that they would always have each other's backs no matter what. They felt grateful for the growth they had experienced in their relationship, and they were excited to see where their future would take them.

9

Unexpected Twists

Emma and Drake's relationship had been going strong for a while now. They had faced many obstacles together, but they had grown closer with each challenge they overcame. They felt like they knew each other inside and out, and they were excited for their future together.

However, one day, Emma received some unexpected news. She had been offered her dream job - as the lead graphic designer for a top advertising agency in a different city. The job was an incredible opportunity for her career, but it would mean leaving Drake behind.

Emma was torn. She had always known that her career was important to her, but she also loved Drake with all her heart. She didn't want to jeopardize their relationship, but she didn't want to miss out on this amazing opportunity either.

Drake could see how much Emma was struggling and encouraged her to take the job. He knew how important her career was to her and didn't want her to regret passing up this chance. They both agreed to try and make it work, even if it meant being in a long-distance relationship for a while.

The next few months were a rollercoaster of emotions for Emma and Drake. They missed each other terribly, but they made the effort to stay connected through phone calls, texts, and video chats. They sent care packages and surprise gifts to each other, just to let the other person know they were thinking of them.

But then, another unexpected twist occurred. Drake's business, which had been thriving, suddenly hit a rough patch. He was struggling to keep it afloat, and it was causing him a lot of stress and anxiety. Emma could hear the worry in his voice every time they talked and knew she had to do something to help.

She took some time to research and came up with a plan to save Drake's business. It involved her moving back to their hometown and working remotely for her new job, while also helping Drake get his business back on track. It wasn't going to be easy, but Emma knew it was the right thing to do.

When Emma told Drake her plan, he was surprised and overwhelmed with gratitude. He knew how much she loved her new job and was touched by her willingness to put it on hold to help him. He also knew how capable and talented she was and had no doubt that she could help him turn things around.

Together, Emma and Drake worked hard to save the business. They poured their hearts and souls into it, and after a few months, they started to see results. They were able to attract new clients and turn around their finances.

Through this experience, Emma and Drake learned that unexpected twists could either tear them apart or bring them closer together. They chose the latter, and it made their bond even stronger. They knew that no matter what obstacles they faced in the future, they could always count on each other to overcome them.

10

The Next Level

Emma and Drake had been dating for over a year now. They had seen each other through good times and bad, and their bond had only grown stronger with time. They had talked about their future together, but they had never really discussed taking their relationship to the next level. That is, until one night when Drake brought up the idea of moving in together.

Emma was taken aback by the suggestion. She had never lived with a significant other before, and the thought of it scared her a little. But at the same time, she couldn't imagine not being with Drake. After some careful consideration, she agreed to give it a try.

They spent the next few weeks apartment hunting and finally found the perfect place. It was a cozy one-bedroom in a quiet neighborhood, and they both fell in love with it immediately. They moved in together and began building their new life under the same roof.

At first, it was an adjustment. They had to learn each other's habits and preferences, and there were a few bumps in the road. But overall, it felt like the natural next step in their relationship. They enjoyed having each other around all the time and being able to share a space.

As they settled into their new routine, Emma and Drake began to think more seriously about their future together. They talked about marriage and starting a family, and the idea of spending their lives together brought them both a sense of happiness and comfort.

But with the talk of a future came some difficult conversations as well. They both had goals and aspirations that they wanted to achieve individually, and they had to figure out how to balance those with their life together. There were moments of doubt and uncertainty, but they always managed to come back to the love and support they had for each other.

They continued to grow and evolve as a couple, building a strong foundation of trust and communication. They faced challenges together and came out stronger on the other side. And through it all, they never lost sight of the love that had brought them together in the first place.

11

The Big Test

Emma and Drake had been living together for a few months now, and things were going well. They had settled into a routine, divided household chores, and found a comfortable balance in their relationship. But then, the big test came.

Drake had to go out of town for a week for work, leaving Emma alone in their apartment. They had spent nights apart before, but never for such a long period of time. Emma was a little nervous about being alone, but she trusted Drake and knew he would be back soon.

The first few days were fine. Emma kept herself busy with work and her hobbies, and FaceTimed with Drake every night. But as the week went on, she started to feel a little lonely. She missed having Drake there to talk to and cuddle with. She found herself looking forward to his return more and more each day.

On the day Drake was set to come back, Emma was filled with excitement and nerves. She wanted everything to be perfect for his return, but she also worried about falling back into old habits of being too dependent on him. She tried to find a balance between being excited to see him and maintaining her independence.

When Drake finally walked through the door, Emma felt a sense of relief wash over her. They hugged and kissed, and she felt happy to have him back home. They spent the rest of the evening catching up and enjoying each other's company.

As the days went on, Emma realized that the time apart had actually been good for their relationship. They had both learned to appreciate each other's presence more, and Emma had gained a newfound sense of independence. They still relied on each other and loved being together, but they also knew they could survive on their own if they had to.

The big test had been a success, and Emma and Drake's relationship had only grown stronger because of it. They were excited to continue building their future together, knowing that they could handle whatever challenges came their way

12

Happily Ever After

Emma and Drake had been together for a year now, and their love had only grown stronger. They had been through ups and downs, but they always came out on the other side even more in love than before. They knew they had found something special in each other.

One evening, Drake surprised Emma with a candlelit dinner at their favorite restaurant. Emma was thrilled, but also a little confused as to what the occasion was. As they enjoyed their meal, Drake took Emma's hand and looked into her eyes.

"Emma, I love you more than anything in this world," Drake said. "You have brought so much joy and love into my life, and I can't imagine spending another day without you. Will you marry me?"

Emma's heart leapt with joy. She had dreamed of this moment for so long, and now it was finally happening. Tears filled her eyes as she said yes, and Drake slipped a beautiful diamond ring onto her finger.

Over the next few months, Emma and Drake planned their wedding. They chose a beautiful outdoor venue and invited all their friends and family. They wrote their own vows, and on the day of their wedding, they stood before each other and professed their love in front of all their loved ones.

As they danced under the stars, Emma felt like the luckiest woman in the world. She had found her soulmate in Drake, and they were embarking on a lifetime of love and adventure together.

Years passed, and Emma and Drake built a beautiful life together. They had two children, a boy and a girl, and watched them grow up into wonderful young adults. They traveled the world and shared countless adventures together, always holding hands and never forgetting the love that brought them together.

As they sat together on their front porch, watching the sunset over the mountains, Emma felt a sense of peace and contentment. They had lived a full and happy life, and had never stopped loving each other. Emma knew that their love would last a lifetime, and that they were truly meant to be together forever.

And so, Emma and Drake lived happily ever after, their love shining bright for all the world to see.

13

The Proposal

Emma and Drake had been together for several years now, and their love had only grown stronger with each passing day. They had talked about getting married before, but neither of them had taken the initiative to propose. That all changed one evening, when Drake decided it was time to take the next step.

He planned a special night for Emma, starting with a romantic dinner at a fancy restaurant. They talked and laughed over their meal, enjoying each other's company as always. After dinner, Drake took Emma for a walk along the beach, holding her hand tightly as they strolled along the shore.

As they walked, Drake stopped suddenly and turned to Emma. "Emma, I love you more than anything in this world," he said, his voice full of emotion. "I want to spend the rest of my life with you. Will you marry me?"

Emma was taken aback by the sudden proposal, but she was also overjoyed. She knew that she wanted to spend her life with Drake, and she said yes without hesitation. Drake slipped a beautiful diamond ring onto her finger, and they shared a passionate kiss under the stars.

Over the next few months, Emma and Drake planned their wedding. They chose a beautiful venue in the mountains, surrounded by nature and their closest friends and family. They spent countless hours picking out the perfect decorations, the best music, and the most delicious food.

On the day of their wedding, Emma was filled with nervous excitement. She slipped into her beautiful white gown, feeling like a princess as her bridesmaids helped her get ready. When she saw Drake waiting for her at the end of the aisle, she felt her heart swell with love.

They exchanged vows under the bright blue sky, with the mountains as their backdrop. They promised to love and cherish each other for all time, and sealed their commitment with a kiss. They danced the night away under the stars, surrounded by the people they loved most in the world.

As they lay in bed that night, exhausted but happy, Emma snuggled up to Drake and whispered in his ear. "I love you, and I always will," she said.

Drake pulled her close, holding her tight. "I love you too, Emma," he replied. "Forever and always." And with that, they drifted off to sleep, content in the knowledge that they had found true love.

14

Wedding Planning

Emma and Drake had been talking about marriage for a while, and now that they were finally engaged, they were excited to start planning their dream wedding.

Emma had always envisioned a traditional wedding with a church ceremony and a grand reception. Drake, on the other hand, wanted a more intimate affair with just close family and friends.

They decided to compromise and settled on a small ceremony at a beautiful outdoor location followed by a reception at a local restaurant. Emma was thrilled with the idea, and Drake was happy to see her so excited.

As they began the planning process, they realized that there were so many details to consider, from the invitations to the menu to the decorations. Emma was a bit overwhelmed, but Drake helped keep her calm and focused.

They worked together to create a budget and started researching vendors. They found a great photographer and florist, and Emma's cousin offered to bake their wedding cake as her gift to the couple.

One of the biggest challenges was finding the perfect dress for Emma. She had always dreamed of a classic, elegant gown, but nothing seemed to fit her vision. After several shopping trips, she finally found the dress of her dreams – a stunning, lace mermaid-style gown with a long train.

Drake was equally nervous about finding the right attire, but after trying on a few suits, he found the perfect one that made him feel confident and handsome.

As the wedding date approached, Emma and Drake became more and more excited. They attended premarital counseling sessions and wrote their vows, expressing their love and commitment to each other.

Finally, the big day arrived, and Emma and Drake were surrounded by their closest family and friends. Emma looked breathtaking in her gown, and Drake couldn't take his eyes off her.

The ceremony was beautiful, and they exchanged their heartfelt vows in front of their loved ones. After the ceremony, they took photos with their families and bridal party before heading to the reception.

The reception was everything they had hoped for and more. The food was delicious, the decorations were perfect, and the atmosphere was filled with joy and love. Emma and Drake danced the night away and celebrated their love with their closest friends and family.

As the night came to a close, Emma and Drake said goodbye to their guests and headed off to their honeymoon destination, excited for the next chapter in their lives as husband and wife.

15

Bachelor/Bachelorette Parties

Emma and Drake's wedding was fast approaching, and their friends wanted to throw them the best bachelor and bachelorette parties. Emma's best friend, Rachel, planned her bachelorette party in Las Vegas. Rachel booked a suite in one of the most luxurious hotels, and the group of girls went to party the night away.

Drake's friends, on the other hand, planned a weekend camping trip in the mountains. The trip involved hiking, fishing, and a lot of drinking around the campfire. It was the perfect way for Drake to unwind before his big day.

While Emma and Rachel were busy partying, Drake and his friends had a wild time in the mountains. But even in his inebriated state, Drake couldn't stop thinking about Emma. He called her at midnight to tell her he missed her and couldn't wait to marry her. Emma was touched by his sweet gesture and told him she loved him too.

The next morning, Emma and Rachel were nursing their hangovers in their hotel room when they received a surprise visitor. Drake had flown to Vegas to surprise Emma and spend the day with her. The girls were thrilled to see him, and they spent the day shopping and sightseeing.

That night, Emma and Drake met up with their respective groups for a joint party. They all went to a club, where they danced and had a great time. It was the perfect end to a memorable weekend.

As the group parted ways and returned home, Emma and Drake couldn't help but feel grateful for their amazing friends and the love they shared. They knew they were lucky to have each other and couldn't wait to start their life together as husband and wife.

16

The Wedding Day

The day had finally arrived. The day that Emma and Drake had been dreaming of for months, the day that marked the beginning of their new life together as husband and wife. They woke up early, filled with excitement and nervousness, knowing that today was going to be a day they would never forget.

Emma's bridesmaids arrived early, and they immediately started helping her get ready. They carefully placed the veil on her head and adjusted her long, flowing dress, making sure every detail was perfect. Emma looked stunning, like a true princess from a fairy tale.

Meanwhile, Drake and his groomsmen got dressed in their perfectly tailored suits. They all looked dashing and ready for the big day ahead. Drake's heart was beating fast with anticipation as he thought about the moment he would see his beautiful bride walking down the aisle.

The ceremony was held in a beautiful garden, surrounded by flowers and greenery. The guests arrived, and the string quartet started playing soft, romantic music, setting the mood for the day. Emma's father walked her down the aisle, and Drake couldn't take his eyes off her. He felt like the luckiest man in the world to be marrying such a beautiful and loving woman.

The ceremony was filled with love and emotion as Emma and Drake exchanged their vows, promising to love and cherish each other for the rest of their lives. Their love for each other was palpable, and their guests could feel it too. It was a moment they would never forget.

After the ceremony, the guests gathered for a reception at a nearby venue. The room was decorated with flowers and fairy lights, creating a magical atmosphere. The guests enjoyed a delicious meal, followed by speeches from the newlyweds' family and friends. Everyone was so happy for the couple, and they all wished them a lifetime of happiness.

Emma and Drake shared their first dance as husband and wife, and the guests joined them on the dance floor. It was a night filled with laughter, love, and happiness. The couple was surrounded by their loved ones, and they felt so grateful for the people who had helped make their wedding day the best day of their lives.

As the night came to an end, Emma and Drake left the venue, hand in hand, and walked towards their honeymoon suite. They couldn't wait to start their new life together as a married couple. They were grateful for their family and friends who had helped make their wedding day the best day of their lives.

As they entered the suite, Emma and Drake looked at each other, feeling overwhelmed with emotions. They hugged each other tightly and kissed passionately, knowing that their love had brought them to this beautiful moment. They were finally together forever, and they couldn't wait to see what their future held. They were excited about the journey ahead, knowing that they would face challenges and obstacles, but they were confident that their love would carry them through everything. They were ready to start the next chapter of their lives, together as one.

17

Honeymoon

After the hectic wedding festivities, Emma and Drake finally got the chance to relax and enjoy their honeymoon. They chose a beautiful beach resort in Bali, Indonesia, where they could bask in the sun, sip cocktails, and take romantic strolls on the beach.

Their first day in Bali was spent exploring the local markets, trying exotic foods, and learning about the local culture. Emma was fascinated by the colorful clothing and intricate artwork on display, while Drake was drawn to the traditional music and dance performances.

On their second day, they took a boat tour around the nearby islands, where they swam in crystal-clear waters and saw dolphins jumping out of the water. It was a magical experience, and they both felt grateful to be able to share it with each other.

As the days passed, Emma and Drake grew even closer. They spent lazy afternoons lounging by the pool, sipping cocktails, and chatting about their dreams and aspirations. They also tried out different water sports, such as snorkeling and surfing, which brought out their competitive sides.

One evening, they decided to take a sunset walk on the beach. As they watched the sun slowly dip below the horizon, Drake got down on one knee and pulled out a small velvet box. Emma's heart skipped a beat as he opened it to reveal a stunning diamond ring.

"Emma, I love you more than anything in this world. Will you do me the honor of becoming my wife?" he said, his voice shaking with emotion.

Tears streaming down her face, Emma nodded her head and said yes. They hugged each other tightly as the sun disappeared completely, and the sky filled with stars.

The rest of their honeymoon was spent celebrating their engagement and planning their future together. They talked about where they would live, what kind of careers they wanted to pursue, and how many kids they wanted to have.

Emma and Drake both felt incredibly lucky to have found each other, and they knew that their love would only continue to grow stronger with each passing day.

18

Future Plans

Emma and Drake spent their honeymoon exploring the beaches and scenic landscapes of a tropical island. As they walked hand in hand along the sandy beaches and watched the sunsets together, they talked about their future plans. They had come a long way since their first encounter and were excited about building a life together.

Emma expressed her desire to start a family and Drake agreed that he was ready to be a father. They talked about the kind of home they wanted to have and the values they wanted to instill in their children. Drake mentioned that he would like to start his own business one day and Emma was fully supportive.

They also talked about their personal goals and ambitions. Emma shared her dream of pursuing a Master's degree in psychology and becoming a licensed therapist. Drake, on the other hand, had always been interested in music and wanted to start a band.

As they discussed their aspirations, they made a promise to always support each other's dreams and aspirations. They knew that they would face challenges along the way, but they were confident that they could overcome them together.

After their honeymoon, they returned to their daily routine, but with a renewed sense of purpose and commitment. They started working towards their individual goals while also taking steps towards building their life together.

Drake started taking music lessons and practicing with his band. Emma applied to a Master's program and started taking classes. They also started looking for a home to buy together and eventually found a cozy little house in a quiet neighborhood.

A year after their wedding, Emma found out that she was pregnant. They were both ecstatic at the news and started preparing for the arrival of their first child. They went to birthing classes together and decorated the nursery with care.

When their daughter was born, they both felt an overwhelming sense of love and responsibility. They worked together to take care of her and adjust to their new roles as parents. They were determined to give her the best possible start in life and make sure that she knew how much she was loved.

As time went on, Emma completed her Master's degree and started working as a therapist. Drake's band started getting more gigs and they even recorded their first album. They continued to support each other in their respective careers and hobbies.

Years went by, and they had two more children. They faced challenges and setbacks along the way, but they always managed to overcome them together. They grew old together, never losing the spark that had brought them together all those years ago.

As they sat on their front porch, watching their grandchildren play in the yard, they reflected on their life together. They had faced adversity, but they had also experienced so much joy and love. They knew that they had been lucky to find each other and to have built a life together. They held hands and smiled, grateful for the journey they had taken and the future they still had ahead of them.

A year after their wedding, Emma found out that she was pregnant. They [illegible] both ecstatic at the news and [illegible] preparing for the arrival of their [illegible] child. They went to [illegible] together and decorated the nursery [illegible].

When their daughter was born, they both felt an overwhelming sense of [illegible] and deep [illegible]. They worked together to take care of her and [illegible] every moment [illegible]. They were determined to give her the [illegible] [illegible] knew how much she was [illegible].

[illegible] degree and [illegible] more gigs and [illegible] continued to support each other [illegible].

[illegible] They loved [illegible] [illegible] to overcome [illegible].

[illegible] adversity [illegible] knew that they had [illegible] each other [illegible] together. They had [illegible].

Check Out :

WRITTEN IN THE STARS: A TEENAGE LOVE STORY

Printed by Libri Plureos GmbH in Hamburg,
Germany